EASY READERS

Pinocchio

by Margaret Hillert

Illustrated by Laurie Hamilton

NORWOOD**H**OUSE 🏠 **P**RESS

DEAR CAREGIVER, The *Beginning-to-Read* series is a carefully written collection of classic readers you may remember from your own childhood. Each book features text comprised of common sight words to provide your child ample practice reading the words that appear most frequently in written text. The many additional details in the pictures enhance the story and offer the opportunity for you to help your child expand oral language and develop comprehension.

Begin by reading the story to your child, followed by letting him or her read familiar words and soon your child will be able to read the story independently. At each step of the way, be sure to praise your reader's efforts to build his or her confidence as an independent reader. Discuss the pictures and encourage your child to make connections between the story and his or her own life. At the end of the story, you will find reading activities and a word list that will help your child practice and strengthen beginning reading skills.

Above all, the most important part of the reading experience is to have fun and enjoy it!

Shannon Cannon

Shannon Cannon,
Literacy Consultant

Norwood House Press • P.O. Box 316598 • Chicago, Illinois 60631
For more information about Norwood House Press please visit our website at *www.norwoodhousepress.com* or call 866-565-2900.

LIBRARY OF CONGRESS CATALOGING-IN-PUBLICATION DATA

Hillert, Margaret.
  Pinocchio / by Margaret Hillert ; illustrated by Laurie Hamilton.—Rev. and expanded library ed.
    p. cm.—(Beginning to read. Fairy tales and folklore)
  Summary: The adventures of a talking wooden puppet who became a real boy. Includes reading activities.
  ISBN-13: 978-1-59953-023-9 (library edition : alk. paper)
  ISBN-10: 1-59953-023-6 (library edition : alk. paper)
  [1. Fairy tales. 2. Puppets—Fiction. 3. Readers.] I. Hamilton, Laurie, ill. II. Title. III. Series.
  PZ8.H5425Pi 2006
  [E]—dc22   2005033500

I want a little boy.
I will make one.
This is the way to do it.
Yes, yes.
I can make a boy.

Look here.
See this and this.
I can do it.
It looks pretty good.

Yes, yes.
Look at this.
Here is my little boy.
Oh, my. Oh, my.

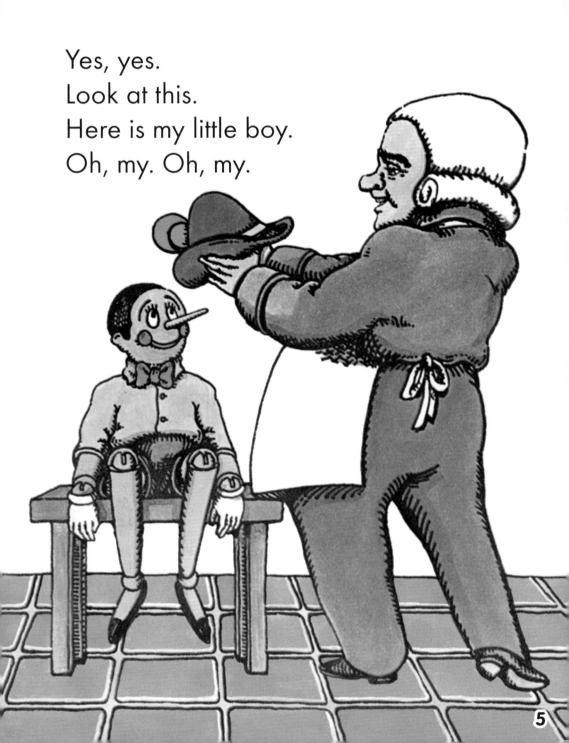

Now, little one, I want you to
go to school.
Boys and girls go to school.
Go on. Go on.
Here are books for you.

Oh, my.
Look at me.
Look at my books.
I will run to school.

No, no.
Do not go to school.
School is not fun.
Come with me to see a play.

Oh, I see something
that looks like me.
What fun!
What fun this is!

Look at you.
I want you to go
with me.
Come here.
Come here.

No, no, no.
I do not want
to go with you.
I will run to my father.

Where did you go?
What did you do?
Where are the books?

I did not go to school.
School is not fun.
I can not find my books.

You have to go to school.
Go on. Go on.
Here is something
to get books with.

What do you have there?
You can do something
good with it.
Oh, come with us and see
what you can do.

Make it go down in here.
Down in this spot.
Good. Good.
Now go away.

Oh, my.
Now get it.
Get it out.
This is for us.
Now run, run, run with it!

Where is my little boy?
Where, oh, where?
I will go look for my boy.

Here I go.
Away, away.
Away in my boat
to find my boy.

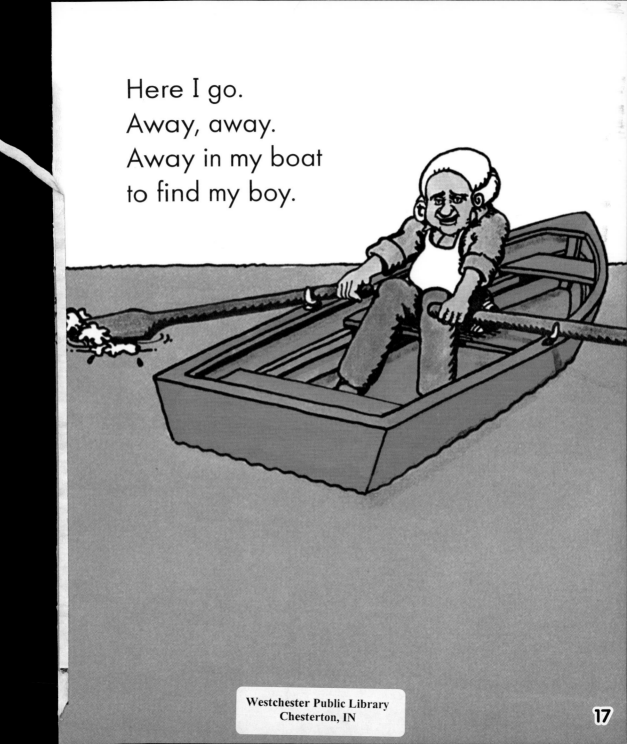

Oh, what is this?
Something big, big, big.
What will it do to me?

Oh, oh, oh.
Here I go.

Here comes something.
Look, look, look.

But what is this?
Look at me now.
What am I?
What am I?

Work, work, work.
I do not want to work.
I do not like this.
I want my father.

You are no good to me.
You do not work.
Get away. Get away.
Here you go.

Oh, look at me now.
But where am I?
What can I do here?

Here comes something big.
It will get me.
In I go.
In I go.
Help, help!

Father, Father.
How come you are here?
Can we get out?

I will help us get out.

Here we go!
We are out now.
We can go to the house.
Good! Good!

You did a good thing.
I will make you
into a boy.
This is how I do it!

Oh, my!
Look at me now.
Do you like me now?
I am a boy, and I
want to go to school.

READING REINFORCEMENT

The following activities support the findings of the National Reading Panel that determined the most effective components for reading instruction are: Phonemic Awareness, Phonics, Vocabulary, Fluency, and Text Comprehension.

Phonemic Awareness: The /p/ sound

Substitution: Ask your child to say the following words without the /**p**/ sound:

pat - /p/ = at	pop - /p/ = op	Pam - /p/ = am
pit - /p/ = it	peel - /p/ = eel	pant - /p/ = ant
pair - /p/ = air	pin - /p/ = in	

Phonics: The letter Pp

1. Demonstrate how to form the letters **P** and **p** for your child.
2. Have your child practice writing **P** and **p** at least three times each.
3. Ask your child to point to the words in the book that have the letter **p** in them.
4. Write down the following words and ask your child to circle the letter **p** in each word:

cap	pail	play	happy	hop	pay	pea
help	sip	stamp	pal	pale	spot	pretty
keep	apple	pen	sample	puddle	carpet	puppet

Vocabulary: Animal Names

1. Ask your child to name the animals in the story. Write the words on separate pieces of paper.

cat	wolf	donkey	whale

2. Read each word to your child and ask your child to repeat it.

3. Mix the words up. Point to a word and ask your child to read it. Provide clues if your child needs them.

4. Mix the words up again. Read the following sentences to your child. Ask your child to point to the word described in the sentence:

- Name the animal in the story that lives in water. (whale)
- Which animal in the story is the only one you could have as a pet living in your house? (cat)
- What animal lives in the forest and has sharp teeth? (wolf)
- Which animal is used to help carry things? (donkey)

Fluency: Echo Reading

1. Reread the story to your child at least two more times while your child tracks the print by running a finger under the words as they are read. Ask your child to read the words he or she knows with you.

2. Reread the story, stopping after each sentence or page to allow your child to read (echo) what you have read. Repeat echo reading and let your child take the lead.

Text Comprehension: Discussion Time

1. Ask your child to retell the sequence of events in the story.

2. To check comprehension, ask your child the following questions:

- What did the man make Pinocchio out of?
- What did Pinocchio do when he was supposed to go to school?
- What happened to the donkey when it fell in the water?
- How did Pinocchio get his father out of the whale?
- Did this story have a happy ending? How do you know?

Pinocchio uses the 72 words listed below.

This list can be used to practice reading the words that appear in the text. You may wish to write the words on index cards and use them to help your child build automatic word recognition. Regular practice with these words will enhance your child's fluency in reading connected text.

a	father	I	play	want
am	find	in	pretty	way
and	for	into	run	we
are	fun	is		what
at	funny	it	school	where
away			see	will
	get	like	something	with
big	girls	little	spot	work
boat	go	looks (s)		
books	good		that	yes
boy (s)		make	the	you
but	have	me	there	
	help	my	thing	
can	here		this	
come (s)	house	no	to	
	how	not		
did		now	us	
do				
down		oh		
		on		
		one		
		out		

ABOUT THE AUTHOR Margaret Hillert has written over 80 books for children who are just learning to read. Her books have been translated into many different languages and over a million children throughout the world have read her books. She first started writing poetry as a child and has continued to write for children and adults throughout her life. A first grade teacher for 34 years, Margaret is now retired from teaching and lives in Michigan where she likes to write, take walks in the morning, and care for her three cats.

Photograph by Glenna Washburn

ABOUT THE ADVISER Shannon Cannon contributed the activities pages that appear in this book. Shannon serves as a literacy consultant and provides staff development to help improve reading instruction. She is a frequent presenter at educational conferences and workshops. Prior to this she worked as an elementary school teacher and as president of a curriculum publishing company.